Dear Parents:

Congratulations! Your child is taking the first steps on an exciting journey. The destination? Independent reading!

STEP INTO READING® will help your child get there. The program offers five steps to reading success. Each step includes fun stories and colorful art or photographs. In addition to original fiction and books with favorite characters, there are Step into Reading Non-Fiction Readers, Phonics Readers and Boxed Sets, Sticker Readers, and Comic Readers—a complete literacy program with something to interest every child.

Learning to Read, Step by Step!

Ready to Read   Preschool–Kindergarten
• big type and easy words • rhyme and rhythm • picture clues
For children who know the alphabet and are eager to begin reading.

Reading with Help   Preschool–Grade 1
• basic vocabulary • short sentences • simple stories
For children who recognize familiar words and sound out new words with help.

Reading on Your Own   Grades 1–3
• engaging characters • easy-to-follow plots • popular topics
For children who are ready to read on their own.

Reading Paragraphs   Grades 2–3
• challenging vocabulary • short paragraphs • exciting stories
For newly independent readers who read simple sentences with confidence.

Ready for Chapters   Grades 2–4
• chapters • longer paragraphs • full-color art
For children who want to take the plunge into chapter books but still like colorful pictures.

STEP INTO READING® is designed to give every child a successful reading experience. The grade levels are only guides; children will progress through the steps at their own speed, developing confidence in their reading.

Remember, a lifetime love of reading starts with a si

For Sam and Polly, who are silly
—A.M.

To all those early readers: keep swimming!
—T.B.

Text copyright © 2021 by Anna Membrino
Cover art and interior illustrations copyright © 2021 by Tim Budgen

All rights reserved. Published in the United States by Random House Children's Books, a division of Penguin Random House LLC, New York.

Step into Reading, Random House, and the Random House colophon are registered trademarks of Penguin Random House LLC.

Visit us on the Web!
StepIntoReading.com
rhcbooks.com

Educators and librarians, for a variety of teaching tools, visit us at RHTeachersLibrarians.com

Library of Congress Cataloging-in-Publication Data
Names: Membrino, Anna, author. | Budgen, Tim, illustrator.
Title: Big Shark, Little Shark, and the spooky cave / by Anna Membrino ; illustrated by Tim Budgen.
Description: First edition. | New York : Random House Children's Books, [2021] | Series: Step into reading. Step 1 | Audience: Ages 4–6. | Audience: Grades K–1. | Summary: "Big Shark is scared! The cave looks far too dark and spooky to swim into. But Little Shark isn't scared in the least! Can he coax Big Shark to explore? Some exciting surprises are waiting deep in the spooky cave!" —Provided by publisher.
Identifiers: LCCN 2020032867 | ISBN 978-0-593-30207-1 (trade paperback) | ISBN 978-0-593-30208-8 (library binding) | ISBN 978-0-593-30209-5 (ebook)
Subjects: CYAC: Sharks—Fiction. | Caves—Fiction. | Fear—Fiction.
Classification: LCC PZ7.M5176 Bj 2021 | DDC [E]—dc23

Printed in the United States of America
10 9 8 7 6 5 4 3 2 1
First Edition

Big Shark, Little Shark, and the Spooky Cave

by Anna Membrino
illustrated by Tim Budgen

Random House 🏠 New York

Here is Little Shark.
Hey! Where is
Big Shark?

Here he is!

Big Shark swims fast!

Why does Big Shark look scared?

Big Shark <u>is</u> scared!
Little Shark wants
to know why.

Big Shark shows
Little Shark
the spooky cave.

Little Shark is
not scared!
Little Shark swims
into the cave.

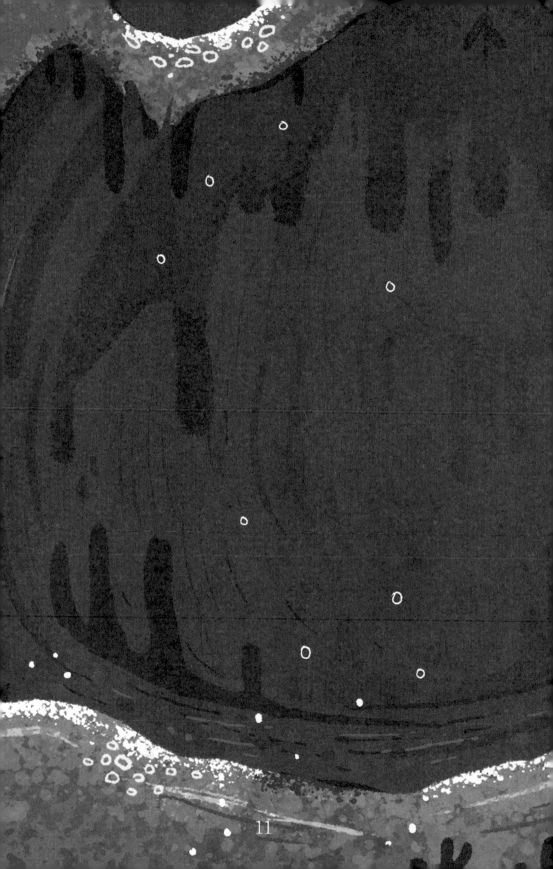

Big Shark does not
want to be alone!

Big Shark follows

Little Shark inside.

The cave is very dark.
Big Shark can not
see Little Shark!

Wait!

What is that?

Is it Little Shark?

No! It is

one vampire crab!

Swim away, Big Shark!

Big Shark wants
to find Little Shark.
Big Shark swims
through some seaweed.

Oh no!
There are two
goblin sharks
in the seaweed.

Swim away, Big Shark!

Big Shark swims away fast.
Then Big Shark bumps into
three scary clown fish!
Ahhh!

Wait.

These clown fish

are not scary.

They are wearing costumes!

Little Shark swims fast
back to Big Shark.
Big Shark is okay!

Big Shark, Little Shark,
and the fish
swim to the end
of the tunnel.

What will they find?

SURPRISE!

It is a costume party!

Now Big Shark is not scared.

Big Shark is having fun!